Dear Michael,

You weren't supposed to see this when I had it sent out in October ... but here it is now in its totally unread splendor.

Peace in the New Year

Paul & Betty
Xmas '69

THE IMAGE

THE IMAGE

by Jean de Berg

Translated from the French
by Patsy Southgate
Preface by Pauline Réage

Grove Press, Inc.   New York

Originally published by Les Editions de Minuit,
Paris, France, in 1956, under the title *L'Image*,
copyright 1956 by Les Editions de Minuit

Library of Congress Catalog Card Number: 66–29270

First Printing

Manufactured in the United States of America
by The Book Press Incorporated

FOR PAULINE RÉAGE

CONTENTS

7

Contents

PREFACE

Who is Jean de Berg?

This question gives me a chance to have some fun at guessing games. First of all, I doubt that a man could be responsible for this volume. It sides far too often with the women's point of view.

And yet it is usually the men who introduce their mistresses to the joys of being chained and whipped, tortured and humiliated. . . . But they know not what they do.

They think, in their naive way, that they are gratifying their pride, or their lust for power, or simply acting out of some innate superiority. To compound this misconception, we intellectual females practically hand them their motives on a silver platter: insisting that woman is free, that she is man's equal, and that she doesn't intend to let herself be pushed around any longer.

9

As though that had anything to do with it!

A man in love, if he has any perception at all, soon realizes his error: he is the master, so it seems, but only if his lady friend permits it! The need to interchange the roles of slave and master for the sake of the relationship is never more clearly demonstrated than in the course of an affair. Never is the complicity between victim and executioner more essential. Even chained, down on her knees, begging for mercy, it is the woman, finally, who is in command.

She knows this only too well. Her power increases directly in proportion to her apparent self-abasement. But, with a single look, she can call a halt to everything, make it all crumble into dust.

Once this is clearly understood by both parties, at the cost of a mutual reappraisal, the game can go on. But its meaning will have changed: the all powerful slave, dragging herself along the ground at her master's heels, is now really the god. The man is only her priest, living in fear and trembling of her displeasure. His sole function is to perform the various ceremonies that center around the sacred object. If he falls from grace, everything is lost.

All this helps to account for the hierarchy of postures to be found in this story, the rituals, the churchlike setting, the fetishism attached to certain objects. The photographs, then, described in great detail, are really nothing more than religious pictures, steps along the way of a new road to the cross.

Like all love stories, this one is about two people. But, in the beginning, one of them is divided in half: one part offering up itself, the other inflicting punishment. Are these not the two faces of our peculiar sex which gives itself to others, yet is conscious only of itself?

Yes, men are foolish to expect us to revere them when, in the end, they amount to almost nothing. Woman, like man himself, can only worship at the shrine of that abused body, now loved and now reviled, subjected to every humiliation, but which is, after all, her own. The man, in this particular affair, stays in one piece: he is the true worshiper, aspiring in vain to become one with his god.

The woman, on the contrary, although just as much of a true worshiper and possessed of that same anxious regard (for herself) is also the divine object, violated, endlessly sacrificed yet always reborn, whose only joy, achieved through a subtle interplay of images, lies in contemplation of herself.

P.R.

I

AN EVENING AT THE X . . .'S

When I saw Claire again for the first time that summer it was at a party given by the X . . .'s, on boulevard Montparnasse. What struck me most about seeing her again was that she hadn't changed at all. I felt as if I had just left her the night before, although in reality I hadn't seen her for at least two or three years, maybe more.

She held out her hand, not seeming in the least surprised to see me, and said, simply, "Hello," exactly as if we had just said good night to each other the previous evening. I said "Hello, Claire," in what I trusted was the same tone of voice, more or less.

Then I said hello to other people, and shook other hands, mostly those of people vaguely connected with the literary or the art world whom I run into almost every week in one place or another. There were certain things I had to discuss with some of them, and plans to make, so that by the time I had finished quite a little time had passed.

There must have been close to thirty people there, spread out among the three rooms that look out onto the boulevard. It must have been June, or the end of May, because I remember one of the French doors was open.

When I caught sight of Claire again she was alone on the balcony outside the open doors, leaning against the railing. She was looking into the room, but not in my direction. I turned to see what she was staring at: it was a group of three people, standing not far from the doors, which consisted of two young men under thirty, whom I didn't recognize, and a very young woman, or girl, in a white dress, whom I didn't know either.

I glanced back toward the balcony and saw that Claire was now looking at me, very evenly. She smiled at me, a smile that might be considered strange, or perhaps it was just the shadows on her face that gave me that impression.

She was leaning up against the railing, her arms out, gripping with both hands the topmost bar.

She was very beautiful. Everyone said that she

was very beautiful. And again, that evening, I thought that it was true.

I went up to the doorway, but not actually out onto the balcony. Claire didn't move. I watched the people going by on the boulevard behind her, strolling along in the warm evening past the brightly lighted windows. I made some inconsequential remark about the scene and Claire seemed to agree, although I couldn't quite make out just what she had said.

I looked at her face and saw that once again she was staring at something, now behind me, in the same general direction as before. I didn't want to turn around to see if it was the same group I had already caught her staring at like this, but I was sure it was since her face had the same expression, that is, no expression at all.

I took a few steps out onto the balcony, which went all the way around the building, until I found myself outside the next pair of doors, these closed. I automatically looked inside between the tulle curtains. Our hostess happened to be standing right inside and said something to me which I didn't catch, not being able to hear it through the glass or make out anything from the movement of her lips. Madame X . . . unbolted the doors and partly opened them to repeat her remark, but the curtains were still in the way so I finally stepped inside. It turned out she had only asked why I was hiding out there, as a sort of joke.

At a loss for conversation, I brought up the subject of the young girl in the white dress, whom I glanced at to show her who I meant. But she didn't seem to know anything about her, or at least wasn't going to tell me. She only said that she was a friend of Claire's, who had come with Claire, and that she hadn't been able to get two words out of her all evening.

In effect, the girl hardly seemed able to answer the two young men who were talking to her. She avoided looking at either of them, and most of the time stared at the floor.

She was attractive, however, with a good figure as far as I could tell, and a pretty face. She was even really quite seductive. Every part of her, despite her extreme youth, gave off an aura of "flesh" which made one think of her far more as a "young woman" than as that ambiguous term, a "girl." And yet, in her little white dress, she looked like a child more than anything else.

Madame X . . . had to leave me, summoned by her duties as a hostess. As I continued to observe the girl, her eyes still lowered, I remembered clearly the

look that Claire had given her. Although I could
not see Claire from where I was standing, I was sure
that she was still on the balcony, leaning back, gripping the railing with her hands. Her expression had
seemed at once intent and empty, the look of one
viewing a rerun of a successful film one has directed
oneself, whose plot couldn't possibly have any sur-
prises.

Claire was very beautiful, as I said, probably even
more beautiful than her friend in the white dress.
But unlike the latter, she had never aroused any real
emotion in me. This astonished me at first, but then
I told myself that it was her impeccable beauty, precisely, her very perfection that made it impossible to
think of her as a potential "conquest." I probably
needed to feel that some little thing about her, at
least, was vulnerable, in order to arouse any desire
in me to win her.

I went over to the open doors as I had done before, but this time with a purpose; and I glanced out
onto the balcony. Claire was not there.

I took a few more steps and looked to the right
and the left: there was nobody on the balcony at all.
Fearing that someone had noticed this maneuver, I
pretended that I needed some fresh air and leaned
for a while on the railing watching the people stroll

along the boulevard past the brightly lighted windows, in the warm evening.

A little later, sitting near a large sofa where a group was in a heated discussion about the latest literary "fraud," I had a chance to observe the girl in the white dress more closely.

The more I looked at her, her features and lines of her body, the more graceful she seemed, gentle and shy, with the movements of a timid ballerina whose slight awkwardness only makes her charm all the more touching. She was passing a tray of refreshments to a group of men who were obviously more interested in her than in helping themselves. Her dress had a full skirt and a fitted waist, with a top that fell off her shoulders, revealing them to be round and gleaming, lightly tanned.

"And what about you, Jean de Berg, you're not taking sides?"

It was X . . . himself dragging me back into the conversation. In turning to face him I suddenly caught Claire's eye. She was watching me, her gaze resting quietly on me. She was leaning against the wall on the far side of the room, smoking a cigarette, alone, away from everybody, next to an empty chair.

She smiled at me briefly, a strange smile that made me think of the first one.

Later that evening, as I was getting ready to leave, I noticed Claire making her way toward me, obviously with something on her mind.

"I'm going," she said. "If you like we could have a drink somewhere, to forget about this dreadful party."

She acted as though she were granting me some favor I'd been begging of her for a long time. I didn't answer right away, not knowing quite how to find out if her young friend would be going along with us or not. But Claire quickly added:

"You can get to know Anne. You'll see, she's very nice."

She stressed the word "nice" in a way that struck me as being rather odd. I raised my eyebrows and asked:

"Anne?"

"Yes, that child there," Claire said, pointing to her although she was just a few feet away, sitting in a chair by herself with her hands crossed in her lap.

I inquired, in my most offhand tone:

"Who is she, anyway?"

"Just a young model," Claire said condescendingly. (Did I mention that she was something of a photographer?)

"And? . . ."

"Well, she belongs to me," Claire said simply.

We were the only people in the back part of the bar where we had settled ourselves. Claire had given our order right away, scarcely consulting me and not even bothering to ask Anne what she wanted: mineral water all around. The waiter served us quickly. Claire took an American cigarette from the pack I had left on the table and lighted it for herself. Then she looked at her friend and, leaning toward her, re-arranged a strand of hair, fine blond hair with highlights of gold.

"She's pretty, isn't she?"

Claire said this as though it were a challenge. I answered, "Yes, very," in a way that could have been merely polite.

"Yes, she's very pretty," Claire insisted, "and more than that, even. You'll see."

I looked at the girl, who hadn't moved a muscle, and kept her eyes lowered on her glass of mineral water, in which little bubbles still rose steadily toward the surface.

"You can touch her, if you like," Claire said.

I glanced at her, wondering if perhaps she were a

little drunk. But she seemed perfectly normal, rather cynical, just the way I had always known her.

"You'll see: it's very pleasant."

I wondered again about her use of the future tense, "You'll see," and again I looked at that smooth, rounded shoulder, tanned against the white material of the dress. My right hand was resting on the back of the booth, and I only had to move it slightly forward to stroke the golden skin with the tips of my fingers. The young girl trembled slightly, and looked up at me for a moment.

"Very pleasant," I conceded to Claire.

Claire quickly added:

"And she has pretty eyes too, you know. Come on, look at the gentleman, so that he can see your eyes," lifting the girl's chin gently, but with her fist closed.

Little Anne looked at me for a few seconds, then lowered her eyes again, blushing. She had beautiful green eyes, it was true, very large, with long curved lashes.

Claire was caressing her face now, talking to her quietly, as though talking to herself.

"A beautiful mouth, too . . . lovely soft lips . . . knowing lips . . . and pretty teeth. . . . Pretty little white teeth . . . come on, let's look at them." She opened her mouth with her fingers.

"Stay like that," she said, her tone suddenly sharp.

Anne stayed as she had been put, like a good little girl, her mouth open to show a row of even, brilliantly white teeth. But it was to Claire that her face was turned.

Her open lips trembled a little, and I thought that she might be about to cry. I looked away, and drank a few swallows of mineral water.

"One day," Claire said, "I'll show you some photographs that I took of her."

At this, I thought I heard the girl object, or moan slightly, at least. She hadn't said a word since her first almost inaudible "Monsieur," accompanied by a graceful little curtsy, when we were introduced. Now I imagined her having murmured "Oh! no," or something of the sort, which made me wonder about the propriety of the photographs in question.

But Claire suddenly showed signs of wanting to leave. As we were all getting up she turned to me again and asked: "Well, how do you like her?" as though I were a prospective customer. At the same time she pushed the girl forward, holding her by the nape of the neck. Then, at point-blank range:

"She doesn't wear a bra, you know. I find it more amusing to make her go out without one."

This time, the girl blushed deeply. I was sure that Claire was going to deliver herself of some new

embarrassing remark about her friend's lack of some
other customary undergarment but, contrary to my
expectations, she refrained and only touched upon
trivial subjects, at least for the rest of that evening.

II

THE ROSES IN THE
BAGATELLE GARDENS

Claire had arranged to meet me the following day: we were supposed to spend the afternoon together in the Bagatelle gardens. She had insisted she wanted to show me the rose garden herself, which I hadn't seen as yet.

I knew enough, by now, not to ask whether we would be alone, or with her young friend.

In the past, when we saw each other, Claire had never expressed the slightest interest in showing me any kind of garden whatsoever, or any of her photographs, for that matter. Up until now she had never made the slightest attempt to meet me outside the various parties where fate would sometimes throw us together for an evening in the same company. For my part, I had never made any effort to lend more warmth to our relationship either. I have already said how little I was attracted by her too perfect beauty, too regular features, her rigidity. I could not recall, either, ever having received the least encouragement for my timid offers to be friendly when we first met, quite the contrary, in fact.

Thinking back, as I waited for her on the terrace of the Royal, I couldn't remember having seen her act differently with anyone else. She was very uninhibited, however, sure of herself, reckless, and purposefully scandalous. But she instantly discouraged any sentimentality as well as, for that matter, any more down to earth proposals she might have the honor of receiving.

On at least one occasion I happened to be present at the execution of one of her suitors. I thought I could discern, at the time, a sort of loathing in the icy, merciless way she did away with him. The scene shocked all of us, back then, for it involved a handsome boy, not without sensitivity or intelligence who, the rumor sometimes went, had been her lover.

It was little Anne whom I spotted first coming toward me. She was wearing the same white dress as the evening before. In order to get by the other customers without disturbing them she wriggled her way between the tables and chairs, raising her arms, swinging her hips like a pretty little dancer. When she finally reached my table she greeted me with her same curtsy, rather ceremonial, the kind they teach to children in religious institutions. And her voice, too, reminded me of a well-behaved young schoolgirl.

"She is here, Monsieur. She is waiting for you in the car."

This pronouncement astonished me, not only because Claire's name hadn't even been mentioned, but also because of the extraordinary respect she gave to the word "Monsieur."

I got up to follow her. Claire's car was parked at a little distance, in the rue de Rennes. Before reaching it I had time to ask the girl several casual questions, but all I could get out of her was "Yes, Monsieur," "No, Monsieur," or "I don't know, Monsieur," as though she were a child.

The car was a brand new 15 CV Citroën. Anne opened the door for me, and I said hello to Claire, who was sitting in the driver's seat. She didn't answer, merely gave a little nod of her head. I helped Anne in, and then got in myself and sat beside her on the front seat where there was just enough room for three people.

Claire started off at once, driving calmly and precisely. In spite of the heavy traffic she made good time, and soon we were out on the less congested boulevards.

It was a beautiful day. Neither woman said a word

but just sat, staring straight ahead. Anne held herself erect, her legs pressed together, her hands clasped on her knees.

I had squeezed over next to the door so as not to take up too much room, and put my left arm behind the girl along the top of the seat. In doing this I accidentally brushed against Claire's shoulder, and she instinctively pulled away. I hastily removed my hand.

Turned, as I was, toward my neighbor, I became aware of her perfume. It was discreet enough not to attract attention, except by being utterly unlike her. But it did seem strong, compelling, very musky, what is usually called sensual, I believe, and certainly not the perfume for a young girl in any case.

I remarked that it was a beautiful day, not speaking to anyone in particular. No one answered. We drove on in silence. I didn't really feel like talking anyway.

We left the car at the entrance to the park, and Claire led us to the rose garden. Once there, instead of letting us wander from flower to flower, Claire made us look at the three or four varieties that she admired the most, knowing exactly where each one was. They were all the same type of flower: large, but not very full, with curled-back petals each quite separate from the other, and a center, or heart, that was still partially closed.

The most beautiful of all, according to our guide, was of a delicate flesh color, darkening near the center where the half-opened petals formed a deep pocket of shadow, making the center appear to be of a much more intense pink.

After a few moments' contemplation, Claire took a quick look around us. We were alone in this deserted part of the garden. The nearest people were about twenty yards away, not looking in our direction, evidently absorbed in a much gaudier display of roses.

When I turned again to my two companions I saw that Claire was no longer looking at the flesh-colored rose, but at her friend who stood, as though frozen, at the edge of the flower bed, her eyes lowered as usual, less than a yard from the flower. I was standing a little back, next to Claire. I looked from the young girl in the white dress to the flower, and back at the girl again.

Claire, beside me, broke the silence.

"Go over to it."

It was a command, given calmly, with no reply expected, by one who is accustomed to obedience. And yet her voice seemed different, lower and more vehement than when she was simply ordering us about the garden or comparing the merits of the various roses.

Anne seemed to know just what was expected of her. After the slightest hesitation she glanced at us to make sure that, where we were standing, we shielded her from the more frequented parts of the garden.

"Come on, hurry up!" Claire told her.

She took a step into the flower bed, her narrow shoes and high heels sinking into the loose earth. I hadn't noticed before what delicate ankles she had. What one could see of her legs was equally admirable.

"Now, go ahead," Claire ordered.

Anne held her right hand out toward the half-opened flower. Very gently she ran her finger tips around the outer edges of the petals, partly closed, barely touching their tender pink flesh. She ran her fingers several times around the closed heart, very slowly. Then she delicately spread open the inner petals and closed them again, using all five fingers.

When she had, in this fashion, spread wide and closed again the flower's center two or three times, she suddenly thrust her middle finger deep inside it, where it almost disappeared entirely. Then she withdrew her finger, very slowly, only to plunge it in again as far as it would go.

"She has pretty hands, don't you think?" Claire asked.

I agreed. In fact, her hand was very pretty indeed, white, little, fine-boned, moving with grace and precision.

Claire was speaking in the same aggressive, cruel tone of voice of the evening before, in the café. With a look of disdain she gestured toward the young girl, who was still attentively caressing the interior of the flower.

"She likes doing that, you know. It excites her. I can prove it to you, if you like. At the slightest provocation she gets all wet. Isn't that right, little one?"

There was no answer.

"All right, that's enough," Claire told her. "Pick it, and bring it over here."

Anne withdrew her hand but then stood motionless, her arms held stiffly at her sides.

I turned back to look down the path we had taken, off the central walk, but nobody was coming in our direction, or paying the slightest attention to us. Claire went on, in an even harsher tone:

"Well, what are you waiting for?"

"I don't dare," said the young girl. "It's not allowed."

One could hardly hear her, she was so afraid of saying the wrong thing. Claire gave me an ironic smile, making sure that I was aware of the stupidity of her protégée.

"Of course it's not allowed . . . neither is walking in the flower beds . . . or touching the flowers. There's a big sign, at the entrance to the park."

Then, more softly, as a mark of sympathy, she added:

"Nothing that I like is allowed either, you know that."

Anne started to reach for the flower's rigid stem but quickly drew back.

"I don't know how to do it," she said all in one breath. "And besides, all those thorns."

"Well, you'll simply have to get scratched," Claire said.

The girl reached out toward the flower's rigid stem, seized it between her thumb and forefinger, and snapped it off. Then she jumped backward and rushed over to Claire as if she were a refuge, holding her trophy in her two fingers.

Separated from its plant, the rose seemed more beautiful than ever. It was perfectly shaped, and the delicate texture of its flesh made one want to feel it, or bite it. Claire condescended to voice her approval.

"Very good. And you see, it wasn't so hard after all. . . . But of course you will be punished, for having hesitated just a little bit too long."

The girl did not dispute this, merely lowered her eyes and blushed in a charming gesture of submissiveness.

I asked, "What are you planning to do to her?"

"I don't know yet. But rest assured, she will be punished in your presence."

Anne raised her face, shaking her head, her eyes full of fear, no doubt wanting to plead for clemency. But her expression changed suddenly and she whispered:

"Some people are coming."

"Well, then, let's be off!" Claire said, indicating the other part of the path.

The girl, who had been hidden from the newcomers by Claire and me, wheeled around and we fell into place on either side of her.

We continued our walk, three abreast, at a leisurely pace. Anne, in the middle, held the rose against her breast. Since there was no one in front of us, no one could detect her crime.

As we passed the mutilated rosebush Claire said to her young friend:

"Look, do you see your footprints?"

Indeed, the imprint of two high-heeled shoes was clearly visible in the loose earth.

We continued our walk, a little faster now.

We soon came to a sort of grove, or thicket, more or less closed off from the rest of the gardens, and completely deserted. Since it was bare of flowers we thought that perhaps here we could find some privacy.

Set back against a dense mass of foliage there were two iron garden chairs which looked fairly comfortable. Claire settled herself in one of them, and waved me into the other.

"Sit down, Jean," she told me. Then, when I hesitated, "The little girl will have to stand. After all, she has to think about where to hide what she has stolen."

Accordingly, I sat down. Anne stood in front of us, elegant and straight in her pretty white dress dappled with sunlight, still holding, both hands against her heart, the flower she had picked. Her eyes were lowered.

We looked at her for a long time, Claire and I.

The cut of her skirt showed off her hips and the slenderness of her waist. Under the top of her dress, with its wide bateau neckline, one could tell she was not wearing a bra. Or was that just my imagination? Claire returned to her subject:

"That rose must be hidden."

It would have looked beautiful against her breast. She could simply pin it to her dress and pretend that she had been wearing it when she arrived. Unless, of course, the sign also said you were not allowed to wear flowers in the garden at all. I pointed out some very thick underbrush on our left:

"All she has to do is throw it in there. No one would ever find it."

"Yes, obviously," Claire said, thinking it over. "But it would be a shame to lose such a beautiful flower. Don't you agree, little one?"

"Yes. . . . No. . . . I don't know," the girl answered.

After a moment of thought, Claire, who was studying her friend carefully, announced:

"It's very simple; you'll just have to hide it somewhere on you."

When the girl didn't seem to understand, since she was neither wearing anything with pockets nor carrying a handbag, Claire was more explicit.

"Under your skirt." She quickly went on, "Here, you'll see. Come over here."

Anne went up to her.

"Lift your skirt," Claire ordered.

At the same time she took the rose from her hands. Anne leaned over to catch the bottom of her skirt and turned the hem up, to show it to Claire, lifting it up to her knees. Claire burst out laughing.

"No, no, little idiot. You're supposed to lift it *all* the way up!"

Anne blushed again, and stole a quick look at me with her wide green eyes.

Then she looked to the right and to the left. She must have been reassured that we were in a relatively safe spot: even if someone came along he couldn't tell what we were actually up to. She turned back to us, holding the edge of her skirt in her hands, and exposed her legs to just above the knees, two round smooth knees on which the stockings were barely visible.

"Hurry up," said Claire.

As though lashed by a whip the girl, in one motion, revealed her thighs to us. Her full, pleated skirt was ideally suited to this operation; one could have raised it up to her face with no trouble at all. The thighs were round and firm, and very pleasingly proportioned. Above the discreetly embroidered tops of her stockings the radiant silky flesh, white and dazzling, was a startling contrast to the narrow black satin straps of her garter belt.

"Higher!" Claire directed, losing her patience.

Little Anne gave me a look of complete despair, this time waiting to see what my answering look would be. Never had her eyes been so beautiful, deep and somber, suffused with terror and surrender.

Her mouth was partly open. Her breasts swelled with her quickened breathing. Just below her waist her hands, which held up the pleated skirt of her dress, were far enough apart from each other to afford an ample view.

As I had thought the night before, she wore no underwear at all, just a simple garter belt of black lace. The short golden pubic hair appeared under this graceful arc, with its narrow little ruffle. The pubis itself was rather prominent, nice and soft, plump, small but inviting.

Again I sought her eyes, but she had closed them. She resembled a sweet and gentle victim, calmly waiting to be sacrificed.

"Well," Claire asked me, "what do you think of it?"

I replied that it all certainly seemed most agreeable. The design embroidered in black on the tops of her stockings, delicate leaves intermingled with tiny roses, I thought was a particularly charming touch.

Claire raised her left hand, which still held the

flower, to the curly pubic hairs and stroked them with the petals. Then she showed me the thin, reddish green stem, about six inches long:

"You see, what we'll do is slip the stem up between the garter belt and the skin about here, close to the crotch. The thorns should be strong enough to hold the flower in place."

"No," I said. "The thorns might be strong enough to tear the flesh, but the flower would fall the minute she started walking."

"Just wait and see," Claire retorted.

She gave the stem a quick going over and it proved to have only one really big thorn, near the end. The rest were brittle little things which she peeled off with her fingernail, remarking:

"See how nice I am? I'm taking off all the prickles, so as not to hurt you."

Then she suddenly turned to me:

"But I forgot, she's supposed to be punished, isn't she?"

Her voice became more authoritative and more loving, as she addressed her friend.

"Spread your legs apart and then don't move. I'm going to hurt you. Come close to me."

Little Anne did as she was told, imploring softly, "No. . . . No. . . . Don't do that. . . . Please don't. . . ."

Claire grasped the rose by its stem end, the blos-

som hanging down, to bring the cruel thorn up
against the most sensitive flesh, on the inner thigh
up close to the pubis. While her victim kept saying,
"No . . . please . . . please don't . . . ," Claire pushed
the steely point slightly into the skin. Anne gave a
little moan and bit her lower lip to keep from crying
out.

Claire waited a few seconds like this, alternately
looking at the face and at the flesh chosen for torture, then in one motion, jabbed the thorn in and
pulled it down. The tender skin was ripped about a
quarter of an inch. Anne gave a cry of pain, from
deep in her throat, and shrank back a step. But she
stayed there in front of us, wide-eyed, open-mouthed
—although trembling all over, her sex exposed.
Claire, leaning back in her chair, contemplated her
victim with what seemed to me to be either hatred,
or the deepest love.

Without making a move, or saying a word, the
two young women stayed facing each other for quite
a long time. Then Anne, who was still holding her
dress up, took a step toward her mistress, coming
back, offering herself again, as close as she had been
before.

A little drop of blood, bright red, had formed on
the naked flesh of her thigh. Claire, whose features
were softening, leaned forward without getting up

from her chair and placed a kiss on each of her hands.

Then, with one finger, she lifted up the edge of the garter belt to the left of the crotch, and with the other hand slipped the stem in under the black material pushing it up towards the hip so that just the flower would show under the filmy ruffle. To keep it in this position Claire just had to push the thorn out to the front where it hooked itself into the lace.

Claire leaned back again to survey the effect from a distance. She put her head to one side and narrowed her eyes, like a connoisseur appraising a painting.

"It's pretty, wouldn't you say?" she asked, pouting at me.

Beneath the central archway of lace the rose, held against the flesh on the left, its head hanging down, spilled out over both the black material and the triangle of blond fur, one of whose upper corners it hid almost completely. The edge of one petal almost touched the beginning of the thigh. Still lower, and to the right, between the lowest point of the triangle where the pubic hairs end in delicate feathers, and the black ribbon of the garter belt, the drop of blood seemed about to run down onto the pearly flesh.

I answered that it was indeed a great success, although perhaps rather overburdened with symbols, in the romantic and surrealist traditions.

Claire smiled. Her face was completely relaxed. Pretending to want to rearrange some small detail, she leaned over her work again. But instead she started to caress the rose just as the girl had done earlier, spreading the petals and plunging a finger into its heart.

She stopped abruptly. Apparently it had only been a game. She had also stroked, briefly, the short curly hair with the back of her finger.

"It's too bad," she said, "that we didn't bring a camera: we could have had a lovely color shot."

She bent down a little and gently licked the drop of blood which was threatening to run down and spot the stocking.

Voices were approaching on the path behind the bushes. Claire had raised her face to look at her friend, a new look, full of tenderness, in her eyes. The two young women smiled at each other a long time.

It was a beautiful day. Anne's golden hair shone in the sunlight. In a peaceful voice that I had never heard her use before, Claire said:

"You may lower your dress."

III

A CUP OF TEA AND ITS CONSEQUENCES

We went to have tea at the pavilion in the park. Claire was lively, talkative, almost childlike. Even Anne spoke with confidence and gaiety. I could see, on this occasion, that she wasn't stupid at all.

However, we only talked about trivial things: gardening, art, literature. Claire made me give the latest gossip on the "fraud" of the moment she had heard me holding forth about the night before at the party. The two young women seemed very amused.

But, little by little, this good mood vanished. The silences grew longer, and Claire's face took on the same closed look it had had at the beginning of our outing. Her classic features, her cold beauty, her remoteness, made me think of some goddess in exile. I saw that she was once again completely engrossed in her young companion, her protégée, her victim, her mirror image. Anne, for her part, had resumed the modest demeanor of an object of lust.

We finished our tea. While Anne was arranging the pleats of her skirt on her lap Claire abruptly asked her:

"Is the rose still in the proper place?"

Bowing her head, she indicated that it was.

"When you're sitting down," Claire went on, "the petals must fall down between your legs and get crushed. Is that right?"

Anne nodded.

"Then you must open your legs wider, so that the flower can hang freely and not be ruined, do you hear?"

The girl, immobile from the waist up, eyes fixed on her empty cup, carried out the order silently and rearranged the pleats of her skirt over her stomach and knees. Claire then asked:

"Can you still feel the petals between your thighs?"

Anne nodded that she could.

"Does it feel nice?" asked Claire.

At this the girl began to blush.

"Well? Can't you answer?"

"Yes, it feels nice," the girl answered.

But it was only a murmur. Claire warned her that if she didn't speak more distinctly in the future she would pull down the top of her dress and expose her breasts, right there in front of everybody. Then, turning to me:

"It would be very easy, you know, since with that gathered neckline her dress is only held up by a band of elastic, and since she hasn't got a thing on under it anyway."

Putting her words into action, Claire reached out and pulled the top of her friend's dress down a couple of inches, enough to bare the rounded shoulder, the beginning of the armpit, and half of one breast.

She didn't dare go so far as to expose the tip, but still, one could see the part that is whiter, softer and more intimate, gently curved, seeming to cry out for more torments. Further up, an irregular red line in the flesh marked where the elastic had been.

"People are looking at us," I said. "You'll have to stop there. What a pity."

"Then let's get out of here," Claire snapped.

We all three stood up. The girl, who had put her dress back in place, went up to Claire to whisper something in her ear. Claire stared at her with an evil smile, apparently pleased to have hit upon a revenge so quickly, and said in a loud voice:

"No, you can't go now. I don't feel like waiting for you. You didn't have to drink all that tea in the first place."

Little Anne followed us out meekly, of course, her head lowered. I didn't have much trouble realizing that she had wanted to go to the bathroom, and hadn't been given permission.

But I didn't know yet what Claire was leading up to. She guided us nonchalantly around the garden making us admire here a flower bed, there a bush pruned in a clever shape, or the design of some walk or other.

At last we came to an area that seemed more wild and natural, where very large trees had blanketed the sparse, unkempt grass with fallen leaves.

This neglected part of the garden would attract no one, especially at that hour when the setting sun was lengthening the shadows. I guessed that our guide was looking for a secluded spot, as far as possible from the rounds of the usual walks.

Claire, indeed, soon stopped, and pointed out a brownish carpet of broken leaves and twigs under a spreading beech tree whose branches, near the trunk, left some space, but then grew down almost to the level of the grass.

"Here is the perfect place," she said. "Don't you think so?"

She had dragged us both in under the tree. On

IV

FALSE STARTS

More than a week went by without my seeing Claire or her friend again.

On the eighth day, quite by chance, I ran into little Anne in a bookstore in Montmartre. She was alone. She pretended not to recognize me, which hardly surprised me, I must say.

I thought of the last image I had of our afternoon in the Bagatelle gardens. The rose must have come loose from the garter belt when the girl knelt down under the beech tree. When she got to her feet again, hiding her face in her hands, I saw the flesh-colored flower lying abandoned on the dead leaves. It had happened to be right under the stream: in the hollows of its bruised petals drops of liquid glistened like pearls. All around it the brown leaves were wet, dark and lustrous.

One large drop had slid slowly down a folded petal of the rose and come to rest on an almost perfect leaf, more or less flat, where the water, before it ran off, had formed a sort of mirror which took several seconds to seep away.

The girl was now speaking to the salesman. What struck me at once was the positive tone, full of assurance, she used in dealing with this man. She wanted a rare book, sold only under the counter, which she asked for with poise, obviously sure that this was the place to find it.

In effect, the salesman soon gave up pretending he'd never heard of it and got a copy out from under the counter. She paid for it without further ado.

I had placed myself in her path, in the middle of the doorway, where she couldn't avoid having to look at me. I said:

"Don't you remember me?"

She regarded me coldly.

"Yes, obviously. But not the way that you mean."

I realized at once that things were going to go very differently that day, so I quickly assured her that I hadn't meant anything in particular, and accompanied her outside.

"What do you want?" she asked me rather rudely.

"Nothing . . . just to talk to you a little . . ."

"I don't feel like having anyone talk to me, and I'm in a hurry. I've got to bring this book back right away."

She showed me the little package wrapped in brown paper: the handiwork of the salesman.

"To whom?" I asked. "To Claire?"

The look in those green eyes became even more hostile: a flashing that was certainly unlike anything I had known before.

"I bring things back to whomever I please. It's none of your business!"

I thought an innocent smile would get me off the hook, and I wished her a pleasant evening.

But she had already turned to go.

This encounter left me highly dissatisfied.

I hadn't imagined that I, personally, would have any power over this girl, but it had seemed only natural that I should continue to enjoy certain privileges, outside of Claire's presence, since they had already been granted to me so liberally, and without my even having asked for anything.

Then, upon further reflection, I began to wonder if I had been granted so much after all, the other day. I was obliged to come to a negative conclusion.

Then I could see how wrong I had been. I could even make fun of my own stupidity, for the recent conduct of little Anne suddenly appeared quite normal and obvious, to the extent that for her to have behaved any differently now seemed impossible.

The situation, in short, had not been what I thought it was.

I felt annoyed and deceived. I decided not to think about those two girls any more, or about the whole absurd story.

I waited for three more days. But, on the fourth, I telephoned Claire.

I am certain that she was waiting for my call although her voice, on the other end of the line, betrayed nothing. In the most banal conversational tone she asked me what I'd been doing, how I'd been feeling "since the last time." I said that I was feeling fine. Then I inquired about her health, and about the health of her friend.

"But . . . which friend are you talking about?"

"Anne, obviously! Are you trying to make a fool of me?"

"Anne! But of course! I'd completely forgotten. If it's Anne you want to see, you should have said so right away. I can lend her to you, my dear, with no trouble at all. You can make love to her as long as you like, if you're in that mood. What day would you like me to send her over?"

There was a brutality in her words that seemed suspicious to me. Affecting complete indifference, I pretended that I thought she was joking and moved away from this burning subject without daring to name a day.

Once I had hung up I thought about my idiotic refusal. I desired Anne very much, that was evident. But I had been afraid to find myself alone with the strange, cold girl of the bookstore who left so few openings I hardly thought I could even carry the thing off. One might as well try and have a go at Claire!

Or was the solution I had adopted, getting out of it entirely, perhaps going to lead to some far more unusual form of pleasure? And was this very hope, without my being aware of it, my real motive?

At any rate it was with Claire that I finally had made a date, at her place on the rue Jacob, on the pretext of wanting to see the photographs she had promised to show me that first day.

I thought again about the girl in the white dress kneeling under the beech tree, about the noise her stream of water made hitting the dead leaves under her dress, and about the rose, its petals all bruised, still dripping with bright beads of liquid.

V

THE PHOTOGRAPHS

I recognized the photographs at first glance: the very ones that were proffered to susceptible souls in the bookstore where I had run into Anne.

It hadn't seemed to me, however, that she was known to the house: or at least not to the salesman who waited on her.

The prints that Claire showed me that afternoon were much larger and far superior in quality to those I had absent-mindedly leafed through one day in Montmartre. At the time, the pictures had struck me as being quite uninteresting, and the poses very ordinary.

This time, on the contrary, I saw them in an entirely new light. It wasn't only because I recognized Anne as the pretty model who had posed for them, either. But I was particularly aware of their extraordinary clarity, while the other prints I had seen hadn't conveyed at all this sense of flagrant reality, more real, more palpable almost, than nature itself.

Perhaps this impression was due to the lighting, or to the dramatic contrast between the blacks and whites which gave added precision to the lines of composition.

In spite of these differences, however, I was sure they were the same pictures. Claire must savor the pleasure of a slave trader in allowing the humiliated image of her friend to be sold to the first customer. And this was, as far as I could tell, the sort of gratification she'd been looking for in me from the beginning.

Used in this fashion, the photographs had a heightened value for me, as well as for her. On top of this, from a technical point of view, I could be quite sincere in offering her my congratulations.

We were sitting at arm's length in two little upholstered chairs before a low table. Above us was an adjustable lamp that must have been used as a spotlight during the posing sessions.

It was the first time that I'd been to her apartment on the rue Jacob. I was agreeably surprised by the ease and cheerfulness of this room and its very modern furnishings (as well as by the rest of the apartment, from what I could tell), especially in contrast to the dark, narrow stairway and the great age of the building.

To achieve this isolation from the world outside, so different in feeling, the heavy curtains at the windows were closed even though it was broad daylight. Even if they didn't open onto a narrow courtyard, as often happens in old buildings, the windows could have only let in a dreary light, less bright yet less intimate than the clever artificial lighting in the room.

Claire handed me the photographs one after the other, first carefully examining each one herself while I was occupied with the preceding one. They were mounted on cardboard the size of regular business stationery. The glossy surface of each was protected by a transparent overlay which one turned back to look at the picture.

In the first one, Anne is wearing a short black slip with nothing underneath but her stockings and a simple garter belt like the one I already admired in the Bagatelle gardens. But these stockings do not have embroidered tops.

She is standing next to a column in the same position Claire made her assume to hide the stolen rose under her dress. Only she is not wearing any shoes and instead of the dress she only has the slip whose thin material she is holding up with both hands, exposing the half-opened thighs and the triangle of her fleece. One leg is straight, the other slightly bent at the knee, the foot only half resting on the floor.

A lace inset decorates the top of the slip but one can't really make it out because it is pulled to one side, the right shoulder strap not being on at all and the left one having fallen off the shoulder. The black lingerie is therefore twisted around, covering half of one breast and freeing the other breast almost entirely. The breasts are perfect, not too full, far enough apart, with the brown halo that encircles the nipple clearly marked but not too large. The arms are well-rounded and gracefully curved.

The face, under the loose curls, is a real triumph: the eyes consenting, the lips parted, a mingled look of ingénue charm and submissiveness.

The lighting, while accentuating the shadows, softens the lines as it defines them. The light is coming from a Gothic window with austere vertical bars, a part of which can be seen in the background at the edge of the picture. The column in the foreground is of stone, as is the window frame, and is about the same width as the girl's hips next to it. Beyond it, at the other edge of the picture, one can see the head of an iron bed. The floor is a checkerboard pattern of very large black and white squares.

The second picture, taken closer up, encompasses the entire bed. It is a single iron bed painted black, stripped of blankets. The sheets are in a state of great disorder. The ironwork of the two upright parts, at the head and foot, is ornate and old-fashioned: metal stems curving and twisting in spirals held together by lighter-colored rings, probably gilded.

The girl is in the same costume lying across the bed on the rumpled sheets. She is flat on her stomach but turned a little, one hip higher than the other. Her face is buried in the pillow, her disheveled hair spread over it; her right arm, bent upward, frames her head; the left arm, at an angle to her body, extends in the direction of the wall. On this side, without the shoulder strap, one can just see the beginning of the breast under the armpit.

The slip is again amply pulled up, this time in the back, needless to say. The waist and the hips are intersected by the black lines of the garter belt. The buttocks are rounded and full, highly evocative. Their firm shape points up some pretty dimples brought into play by the asymmetry of her position. The thighs are opened to a hollow of darkness. The left knee, bent way up, disappears under a fold of the sheets while the foot touches the extended right leg.

The picture is taken from fairly high up so as to display the buttocks in the most accommodating position.

In the next one the girl is entirely naked, hands chained behind her back, kneeling on the black and white checkerboard floor. The picture is taken in profile and also from above. One sees nothing but the girl, kneeling naked on the floor, and the whip.

Her head is lowered. Her hair falls on either side of her face, hiding it, exposing her neck which is bent down as far as it will go. The tip of one breast appears below the shoulder. The thighs are together, leaning backward, and the trunk is bent forward in a way that makes the buttocks protrude most fetchingly as they await their punishment. The wrists are bound together behind the back, at waist height, by a slender chain of shiny metal.

A similar chain ties the ankles one against the other. The whip is resting on the squares of the floor not far from the little upturned feet, the soles of which one can just see.

The whip is of braided leather like those that are used on dogs. From the thin, supple tip it becomes progressively thicker and harder up to the part that one holds in one's hand, which is almost rigid, forming a sort of very short handle. The lash, motionless on the floor, delineates an S whose narrowest tip curves back on itself.

The girl is still naked and on her knees, chained now to the foot of the bed. One sees her from the rear. The ankles are closely bound together but crossed, one foot over the other, which forces the knees wide apart.

The distance between the two hands is much greater, however, on either side of the blond head and at the same level. The arms are held almost horizontally, the elbows bent at a right angle toward the front. The wrists, still with the same metal chains, are attached to either end of the top bar of the iron bedstead.

The trunk and the thighs are held straight without the least bending of the hips. But the whole body is slightly twisted to one side, due to the fatigue caused by this position. The head hangs forward and to the right, almost touching the shoulder.

The buttocks are marked in every direction by deep lines, very clear and distinct, which crisscross the central crack, more or less stressed according to how hard the whip fell.

This picture of little Anne chained to her bed, on

her knees in a most uncomfortable position, is obviously more moving because of the cruel evidence of the torture she has undergone. The black ironwork forms a pattern of elegant arabesques behind her.

The nude girl is bound to the stone column by thick ropes. She is facing the camera, her legs open, her arms raised. A black band covers her eyes. Her mouth is screaming, or else distorted by the extremity of her suffering.

The ankles are tied to the pillar on the right and on the left, diametrically opposite each other, so that the legs are wide apart, the knees slightly bent. The arms are pulled up and back, only visible up to the elbows. The hands, no doubt, are tied together behind the pillar.

The ropes bite deeply into the flesh. One goes under the right armpit and across to the other side of the neck, imprisoning the whole shoulder. Others are tied around the arms and the ankles. Others, finally, hold the legs above and below each knee so as to force them back against the stone and as far apart as possible.

The tortured body, whose reflexes clearly show that it is struggling against its bonds, has two deep wounds from which blood flows freely.

One extends from the tip of the breast to the arm-pit, on the side where there are no ropes. The blood pours down one whole side in little rivers of varying force which run together and separate again in an elaborate network which covers one hip and a good part of the stomach. It even flows into the navel and the pubic hair in a thick stream which runs down the belly.

The second wound, in the lower part of the body, ornaments the other side. It pierces the groin just above the pubis, penetrating the lower belly and curving down to the inner part of the thigh. The blood from this wound flows in large rivers, almost covering the whole area, running down to the rope which binds the body above the knees. There it accumulates a moment and then pours out directly onto one of the white flagstones where a pool has formed.

This picture, extremely fascinating in its horror despite the somewhat romantic exaggeration, could only be the result of a trick. The two wounds and the quantities of blood undoubtedly had been faked by using red paint on Anne's obliging body. But it was done so well that one could easily be fooled, especially since the contortions of the victim were quite convincing.

Perhaps it was the meticulous way the streams of blood had been designed, and their too obvious fluidity, that gave the whole thing away. In any case, far from obscuring the harmonious lines of the body, they seemed to give it a new beauty.

The last photograph was a logical conclusion. The tortured body of the girl, apparently lifeless, is stretched out on the black and white checkerboard floor. She still wears nothing but the black band across her eyes.

She is lying on her right side, the upper part of her body half flung back so as to turn her face up into the camera. The right arm is stretched the length of her body while the left arm is raised over her head hiding the ear but giving a good view of the downy armpit and the breast.

The legs are bent, the right one slightly and the left much more, the knee pulled way up. From the way the picture was taken and the lighting, one can clearly see the inside of the right thigh, the buttocks, the lower pubic region and all the surrounding tender flesh.

The amount of blood which gushes from the central wound, flowing onto the upper thigh and the floor on either side of it, gives the impression that the girl has been fatally stabbed, or something of that nature.

Blood trickles out of her half-opened mouth and down her cheek before dripping to the floor. Apart from this detail the face seems peaceful, almost happy. One might almost think, for a moment, that the mouth is smiling.

I noted that this photograph was not taken on the same day as the others, or as some of the others. The paint which had spotted the breast could, of course, have been washed off since the previous shot; but missing entirely were the whip marks on the buttocks which do not, naturally, disappear that fast. Perhaps, then, the pictures had been taken in a different order? Or perhaps those charming stripes across the skin had just been make-up, like the rest of it?

I was about to ask Claire when, turning to her, I noticed that she was holding still another photograph she must have taken from her folder just when I thought the series was finished.

She handed it to me. Right away I could tell that it was different from the others. The way it was taken, in the first place, was not at all the same, but there were other things. The body was partially cut off by the camera, while before it had always been shown in its entirety. The setting, moreover, was no longer the austere Gothic room but the very room that we were sitting in. Thrown back in one of the little armchairs a woman, her nightgown raised to her waist, is caressing the interior of her sex.

Because of the blurred folds of the nightgown one can only distinguish the naked parts: the two arms, the hands, the lower belly, and the opening of the thighs. The legs from the knees down, as well as the head, are not in the picture.

In the gaping crevice of the thighs the index and the middle fingers of the left hand part the lips on one side, on the other the thumb and little finger of the right hand perform the same function. The fourth finger of this hand is bent back; the index finger touches the tip of the clearly erect clitoris; and, lower, the middle finger readily penetrates the opening up to the middle joint. Under the intense lighting the surface of the mucous membranes glistens from its secretions.

What gave me the final proof were the dark, polished fingernails of those two hands. I remembered that Anne left her fingernails natural. And then something about the whole position, the curve of the arms, every detail of the pose, seemed less abandoned, less pleasurable, and the pubic hair a little darker. I glanced at Claire to ask her if I knew the model she had used this time.

Her face was no longer the same: somewhat flushed, less cold, visibly troubled. The general effect made her seem infinitely more desirable than she had ever been before. She was wearing a black sweater and fitted pants; thrown back in her chair, as in the photograph, she let her hand wander in the hollow of her thighs. The polish on her fingernails was an intense red.

I realized at once it was a picture of herself that she had shown me. She had probably used an automatic time release to take it. The voluminous nightgown, the absence of the face: it was all calculated so that she could add this shot to the others without anyone suspecting it was of a different person.

I put the photograph down on the table without taking my eyes off Claire, wondering if I should approach her.

But Claire got hold of herself immediately. She sat up abruptly in her chair and wheeled around, once again looking like her usual self: severe, rigid, flawlessly beautiful.

She didn't say a word. She just stared at me, straight in the eyes, rather haughtily, to see if I was going to say anything.

77

I said, gesturing toward the table: "That last photograph there, is that still Anne?"

"Who else could it be?" she answered dryly, in a tone that did not invite me to pursue the matter.

VI

AN EXPIATORY SACRIFICE

Claire put the photographs back in their folder. She seemed dissatisfied. I couldn't figure out how to bring her back to that brief wordless scene that had taken place over the picture of her body (that it was her body I was by now absolutely certain). The state she had been thrown into, for a moment, by the idea that a man saw her in such a posture, open, aroused, indecent, seemed to suggest new possibilities that would have been unthinkable judging from her usual behavior.

But when she asked me, with condescending politeness, what I thought of her talents as an executioner I felt once more how incapable I was of seducing her, or of even wanting to.

Little Anne was enough to satisfy her need to humiliate someone. She offered her to others as a beast of prey might share its kill, instead of offering herself.

I answered that I thought her talents as an executioner were on a level with her talents as a photographer, and that that was a great compliment.

"Thank you," she said, bowing to me with an ironical little smile.

But all this lacked gaiety or spontaneity. Having recovered from an inexplicable moment of weakness Claire was on the defensive, ready to bite. I had the impression that she was now looking for a chance to demonstrate her strength, or her hardheartedness.

"And my model, aren't you going to compliment me about her?"

I decided to answer referring only to Anne, and assured Claire that in Anne she indeed possessed the most delectable of victims.

"You ran into her the other day, didn't you?" she then asked me.

"Yes, in Montmartre. Only she wasn't being delectable at all!"

"Oh? What do you mean?"

I thought for a second, trying to make out what Claire knew of our encounter.

"She probably just didn't feel like talking," I said evasively.

"Did she, by any chance, show a lack of respect for you?"

"I didn't know she owed me any."

And I smiled, amused by this idea.

"She owes it to you, if I so desire," said Claire.

That's just what the situation proved to be, from then on. There was only one problem: to guess exactly what it was that Claire desired. Many things, no doubt, provided they were carried out in her presence.

As for me, it was mostly curiosity that kept me there, at that particular point. But as soon as Anne came into the room, summoned by her friend in a voice full of menaces, or perhaps promises, I was aware of the reawakening of certain other feelings.

We had sat back down, Claire and I, in the two little comfortable armchairs facing the middle of the rug. The low table, of no use now, had been pushed into a corner.

Anne therefore had to appear before us, according to the custom: standing up, arms at her sides, eyelids lowered. She was dressed in a pleated skirt and a blouse; not wearing shoes, she walked in her stocking feet. She had been called in to straighten out the incident at the bookstore and to be punished on the spot if she deserved it.

Naturally, it wasn't a question of knowing whether the girl deserved a punishment or not, but of finding an excuse to torture her as we pleased while seeming to punish her. Claire, moreover, was speaking with a vehemence that seemed to bode no good for her victim.

It only took a few seconds to convince her that there was evidence of grave insubordination on Anne's part. And her immediate punishment was decided before she could even open her mouth to defend herself.

"Get undressed!" Claire ordered.

Little Anne seemed to know her role by heart, and needed no directing. She got to her knees in front of her mistress, on the thick wool carpet, and took off her clothes one by one. To all appearances she was observing a sort of ritual.

Since it was very hot she wasn't wearing much of anything anyhow. She started with her skirt which she unhooked at the waist, opened at the hip, and pulled up over her head.

She wore no panties that day either, and her garter belt was of pale blue satin with a little lace flounce. She unbuttoned her short blouse and left it that way, partly open, so that one could already glimpse her breasts under the light material.

'Then she undid her stockings and removed them, one after the other, lifting first one knee and then the other. Then she unhooked her garter belt in the back and placed it, along with the skirt and the two stockings, beside her on the rug.

Having finally removed her blouse, the last piece of clothing, she raised her arms in the air to hide the upper part of her face behind them.

She stayed in this position, kneeling, thighs spread apart, very straight, entirely exposed for us to contemplate.

Her body was soft and full, still childishly thin but nicely rounded and dimpled, more touching than I had ever seen it. The fair skin was very smooth all over, a little paler on the belly and the breasts whose pink tips seemed to have been lightly rouged. Even though I was looking at the young woman from the front, I was reminded of the picture that showed her from the back, chained to the iron bed in a similar position, the buttocks streaked by the lashes of the whip. The memory of those photographs and their tortures gave full significance to the attitude of waiting in which the victim held herself.

Claire seemed ready for any sort of violence. But she confined herself, at first, to several comments on the charms of that docile body, the perfection of its shape, the gracefulness of the attitude, lingering over eulogies for the firm breasts and the plump little sex, extolling that soft flesh offered up for her amusement, the fragile skin that she already savored mutilating.

Far from softening during these preliminary remarks, her voice grew more violent and more enraged as she proceeded with the program of the coming tortures. As far as I was concerned, even the most fantastic of tortures sounded perfectly ordinary compared to those I had just seen such lifelike reproductions of in the photographs.

Claire interspersed her speech with specific, obscene words, with insults, and with degrading intimate references. At the height of her passion she suddenly stopped. . . .

After quite a long silence she said, more calmly: "Get up, you little slut! Go and get me the whip!"

The girl stood up, keeping one arm over her eyes. She turned and crossed the rug to the door. She moved with a childlike grace that was rather disconcerting, considering her utter nakedness. The two round shapes of her buttocks, as yet unharmed, undulating as she walked, held out promise of the most ruthless pleasures.

Anne came back right away, one of her forearms still hiding the upper part of her face. In her free hand she held a leather object. She knelt again before Claire, close enough to hand it to her. It was the same braided whip as in the photograph. Claire seized it by the handle and made the victim turn a little more sideways, in front of her chair, so that I could get a front view of her myself. Without having to be told anything further, the girl once more spread her knees wide and raised her arms, this time above her head so that we could also watch her lovely frightened face and her pretty, half-opened mouth during the torture.

But Claire, instead of striking, seemed now to grow gentler. She spoke in a softer voice. Although her remarks still dealt with various atrocities in some detail, one might have mistaken them for words of love.

The girl was within easy reach. Claire leaned forward and held out her left hand to run her fingers several times over her breasts. The little pink nipples stood up, erect. Claire began to play with them, to make them even stiffer, then she stroked the hollow of the armpit nearest her.

Her hand came back to the breast again, then descended the length of the hip to come and stroke the insides of the thighs. Her voice was syrupy, as though she were talking to a little child.

"She's adorable like that, the little girl. She loves it when we put her on her knees so we can whip her, doesn't she? . . . It gets her all excited. . . . She is all wet already, isn't she? . . ."

The inquisitive hand went up again until it reached the sex. The fingertips stroked the crevice two or three times, moving from front to back. At the same time the other hand, which held the whip, caressed the buttocks from behind.

Then abruptly the index finger of the left hand penetrated between the lips, below the curly hairs of the crotch. The finger entered with a single thrust into the ardent depths. Anne closed her eyes entirely and opened her mouth a little wider.

Claire gave me a triumphant look. The ease of penetration proved, in effect, that the girl was nice and moist, aroused, ready for love.

"You see," Claire said to me, "how well she has been broken in: when one is about to beat her, she gets all set for her orgasm. It's a question of training, just like with a dog! I only had to fondle her often enough in this position, and now she can no longer keep herself from wanting to be satisfied. . . . Isn't that so, you little whore?"

At this, without taking her left hand out from between the thighs in front, Claire, with her right hand, administered a violent stroke of the whip across the girl's buttocks. Her skill in wielding the lash indicated long hours of practice.

The girl jumped, her arms instinctively dropping

a little. But she quickly raised them again. Claire struck a second time.

"Look at Jean," she ordered. "It's at his request that you're being punished."

Anne raised her eyelids, even holding them wide open in order to be able to bear the pain more easily. She also concentrated on keeping her mouth open.

To be able to hit harder and more conveniently, Claire was obliged to remove her left hand from the girl's sex. The blows, better aimed, fell with regularity across the small of the back. Now the girl gave a little groan each time the whip landed, an "Oh!" of pain that sounded like a gasp of love.

Claire went on beating her, faster and faster. The rhythm of the victim's cries mounted: "Oh . . . Oh . . . Oh . . . Oh. . . ." Then, unable to bear it any longer, she dropped one arm until it touched the floor and sank back, half sitting on her legs.

Claire stopped the beating. The girl, seized with terror, straightened up again, correcting the position of her knees, and raised her arm once more above her head.

"It might be better to tie her up," I said.

"Yes, if you like," Claire answered.

Then, very quietly, the girl began to cry. The tears formed in the corners of her eyes and rolled down her flushed cheeks. A shudder ran through her body from time to time. Then she tried to sniffle, as inconspicuously as possible.

Kneeling on the thick wool rug, perfectly straight, thighs well apart, hands held in the air, she didn't even dare wipe away the tears which ran slowly down her face.

We sat there for a long time, looking at her.

Again it was little Anne who had to go and fetch the shiny metal chains. With their heightened coloring, her martyred buttocks seemed even more disturbing than before.

As soon as she returned, Claire, who had gotten up from her chair, brutally pushed her back down on her knees, on the excuse that she hadn't carried out the order quickly enough. With one hand she held her victim's wrists together behind her back and with the other slapped her with all her might, four or five times.

The girl began to cry twice as hard. Without paying the slightest attention, Claire made her come over to me, under the whip, dragging herself on her knees from one edge of the rug to the other. Once there, she put the chains around her wrists and ankles.

The chains were made up of sturdy links of chrome-plated steel, finished at one end by a larger ring, and at the other by a hook with an automatic lock. One simply passed the hook through the ring to make a loop to hold the limb, twisted it once or twice around a support, and locked the hook onto whatever link it reached to.

This system was fast and convenient. In a few seconds the girl's hands had been chained to the two arms of my chair which, in the way they were detached from the seat, seemed almost designed for this purpose. The ankles, then, were linked together, one foot crossed over the other, the same arrangement I had admired earlier in the photograph, which made it impossible to bring the thighs together. The girl, furthermore, was obliged to lean over me, her chest between my knees, her blond head coming closer to meet my hands.

Very gently I caressed her tear-stained face, letting my fingers wander over her neck and breasts, her shoulders, underneath her arms. Then I asked Claire to go on with the punishment. But the renewed whiplashes, landing on the bruised buttocks, only made the girl cringe feebly.

Claire seemed satisfied, for the moment, to see her friend so powerless. She applied the whip more listlessly, more cautiously, almost with a kind of affection.

I took the delicate neck in my hands again and forced little Anne to hold her face up to mine. I leaned down to her mouth and kissed her. Her lips melted under mine. I drew back at once and, tightening my hold on her neck, told her:

"You'd better treat me better than that, you little slut."

I began to kiss her again. Her obedient lips and tongue began moving pleasurably under mine, as the whip cracked more sharply now on the naked flesh.

As I guided the docile neck down between my thighs I noticed that Claire had put a little pillow next to us on which she was kneeling, one leg bent. She had dropped the whip, and her right hand carefully caressed the two rounded shapes, marked with bright red stripes, which I could view myself in a very pleasant perspective from above.

The knowing hand moved toward the sex, from the rear, and once again disappeared into the crevice. I could hear Claire murmuring: "She is soaking, the little darling . . . ," and after a while: "It's a real lake." Her thumb, easily finding the orifice, sank in up to the hilt, withdrew, and plunged in again. Anne began to moan.

Her moans got longer, and harsher, as the caress continued, the hand moving to and fro between her thighs.

From where I was sitting I couldn't follow the exact movements of the fingers, but whatever they were, judging from the mounting cries of the girl, the undertaking was about to be crowned with success.

For my part, I was content at first just to play with the moist mouth and the tips of the breasts, while contemplating the lovely buttocks surging back and forth now with an insistent rhythm.

Then it occurred to me that Claire was not so naive as not to realize what irregularities she was exposing her friend to in presenting her to me in this position. I took out my own organ and held it to the lowered face of our prisoner.

Shrinking back at first, she finally abandoned herself, even to rounding her lips indulgently and skillfully. Without any doubt this was not her first experience. I put my hand on the back of her neck to lightly guide the upward and downward movement of her willing head.

When I felt that the little bitch was about to reap the fruits of her labors I shouted to Claire:

"Whip her again, now!"

Claire leaned back, one knee on the pillow, and began to whip the chained girl furiously, aiming her blows at the most sensitive areas, the inside of the thighs and the region between the anus and the vulva, which made the poor thing jump convulsively and utterly delightfully.

To insure complete control I grasped the blond head firmly with both hands so that I could immobilize it, or move it up and down, up and down, according to the dictates of my pleasure.

VII

THE FITTING ROOM

At the close of this last session Claire informed me that in the future I could have little Anne whenever I wanted her, and could amuse myself with her however I pleased. Any time I judged that she hadn't been sufficiently obliging, or, simply, if a clumsy move on her part hadn't been quite to my taste, she would be severely punished.

These arrangements, made in the presence of the interested party in a bar near Saint-Sulpice, suited me admirably.

I didn't even feel any pressing need to exercise my new prerogatives right away. In the days that followed we were content just to have dinner together, the three of us, in various restaurants of the quarter whose inner recesses provided some degree of privacy, so that I could sample, from time to time, the least offensive of my privileges. Claire watched the progress of her pupil with a critical eye, progress in the art of becoming a perfect slave.

97

Sometimes the inquisitive look of a waiter or of an astonished customer would interrupt one of our wordless little scenes, or bizarre remarks. . . . The hint of scandal, which only deepened Anne's embarrassment, added immeasurably to our own passions.

If by chance these practices aroused me beyond control I always had recourse to the car, parked in some deserted street, where I would have the girl caress and fondle me.

One afternoon that week her mistress even let me have her all to myself: I was to take her shopping for various items of lingerie which I was charged with selecting for her.

Claire preferred narrow lace waistbands and stockings with embroidered tops. As for brassieres, she would only tolerate the skimpiest models which support the breast from underneath without covering it entirely, leaving bare as much of the nipple as possible. Since Anne was not supposed to wear either panties or a slip, we were limited to these three articles.

I thought at once that the fun would lie in the trying on of these garments. But when I noticed in the window of a store on the Faubourg Saint-Honoré the charming features of a salesgirl, it came to me that such a ceremony could be far more lively than I'd imagined. Having learned from Claire that Anne had been savagely beaten that morning (for a very minor mistake, by the way) I could already picture her shame in front of the astonished fitters whom I would call, on purpose, for a consultation.

Claire had given me no further instructions, so the whole thing was up to me. If she preferred not to come with us it must be that she didn't want to complicate matters: a couple always seems less suspicious and naturally is more self-assured. All we needed was an amenable salesgirl: young and pretty as they often are in the better stores, and not too easily shocked. She should not, however, bring an overactive complicity to her services, but should simply be a witness, understanding yet discreet.

This one seemed to fit the bill. The store was quiet and luxurious, and displayed many delectable models. The young woman who was waiting for some customers behind a showcase of pink slips on hangers must have been twenty-five or thirty. She was a brunette, and had a nice figure. Seeing me looking at her, she gave a little smile of encouragement: it is always wise to encourage a man who wants to buy feminine underthings. We went in.

The pretty salesgirl turned to my companion to ask what we wanted, but it was I who answered, pointing to a white nylon garter belt that was shown in the window. Anne, as usual, held her tongue and lowered her eyes.

The item was therefore presented to me for inspection, along with several other similar models. I gave my opinion on certain details of their respective lines, making clear which ones I thought were most suitable, and stressing the necessity for wide openings both in front and in back. The salesgirl smiled understandingly, and then went on to discuss the quality of the various garments.

Our conversation was perfectly natural and pleasant. She didn't seem to wonder too much about the self-effacing behavior of my companion.

"This," I said, "is in a sense the most amusing one. But it comes down a little too far: I'm afraid it won't completely uncover the triangle, you know, at the lower part of the stomach."

The woman looked at me. Then she glanced at Anne and looked back at me.

"That *is* a drawback, wouldn't you say?" I added.

"It's really very comfortable to wear, sir."

"I don't mean to wear, of course. I mean it might interfere with the view . . . and with the hands, as well."

This time her smile was much less professional.

She even blushed a little. I turned to Anne and said:

"I think you'd better try it on."

Anne answered, "Yes, if that is your wish," but a little too softly, and I'm not sure if the girl understood the implications of the phrase.

I said that we would take the opportunity to try on, at the same time, a matching bra, and I described the sort of thing I was looking for. The salesgirl unhesitatingly brought out the most indecent things she had.

Having made my selection, on the pretext of wanting to show her the garter belt with the ruffle that Anne was wearing, I calmly lifted Anne's dress up above her thighs:

"This is what I mean, you see. . . ."

The pretty salesgirl stared at me in amazement, finally, and then turned her glance to the smooth, firm flesh I was showing her.

"Yes, I see," she answered simply.

I asked Anne to hold up her dress herself while I explained the intricacies of lace ruffles hiding the elastic, using both hands to stretch them out in my demonstration.

"Pull your dress up higher," I told her, "and come closer to the light."

She obeyed me immediately. The girl, who had been leaning over to watch, had plenty of time to note that her young client wore no panties. She must even have been able to smell the penetrating perfume Claire made Anne put on her blond pubic hair.

While Anne was getting undressed to try on the garter belt and the bra in the fitting room, I stayed outside with the salesgirl talking about the weather. She entered quite freely into this most ordinary conversation, but her expression still had something bemused, and curious, about it. I saw that we could go further.

I turned toward the fitting room:

"Hello, are you ready yet?"

There was no answer.

I went on, in a benevolent, fatherly tone: "Well, now, let's come have a look at you. . . ." and I headed for the closed curtain which I opened to join Anne.

She was quite charming, all in white. She had on only the new bra and the garter belt, each more delightfully immodest than the other. I pulled her close to me to kiss her.

After a few moments I decided to call the salesgirl. I stuck my head out between the curtains:

"Would you mind coming here for a minute, please?"

She came over smiling bravely, looking me straight in the eye.

The room was large enough for three people. Anne was at the other end, facing us. The salesgirl stood beside me. Anne held her arms out from her body so that we could see the effect more easily. Instinctively she had half opened her mouth and parted her knees. I held one of her wrists up higher and made her turn slightly, to the right, and then to the left.

"As you can see," I said, "they both will do. But I think you should take in the belt a little."

The young dark-haired woman went and put her finger between the nylon and the hollow of Anne's waist. I had the impression that she was really beginning to be affected by this unusual spectacle.

"Turn around!" I ordered Anne, letting go of her wrist.

She hid her face in her hands and turned. The two round globes of her buttocks were crisscrossed by a dozen red lines which stood out clearly on the delicate skin. As several hours had passed since her punishment, the general discoloration had faded and only the marks of the whip itself were visible on the blond flesh.

I looked at the pretty salesgirl but she no longer dared to look at me, transfixed by this sudden revelation and, as it were, touched by its grace. Her arm, held out to adjust the hooks at the waist, had paused midway between herself and the revered object which she was now afraid even to touch.

Upon closer examination the red marks did not seem to be uniform: the leather lash had left a series of dotted lines which corresponded to the bulges in the braiding, wounding the flesh unevenly. Claire must have hit very hard. Certain of the stripes still stood out clearly. . . . I couldn't help lightly running my fingertips over them to get a better idea, or to make Anne feel more deeply the ignominy of her condition, or to comfort her for having suffered so much. . . .

"It's nothing," I said to the salesgirl. "Don't give it another thought. She was whipped a little, because she wasn't a good girl, that's all."

We joined our friend again at five o'clock in a very dignified tearoom where several old ladies conversed together in hushed voices.

Claire, who was waiting for us, had chosen a table in the most propitious corner of the room. The pleasure I felt on seeing her astonished me, but then

I realized that this day, unless I had seen her, would have been incomplete, would have even been of no value at all.

All I said to her was that she was beautiful, which was quite a thing for me to say.

She looked at me silently. She seemed to understand something, something far away, and she smiled at me mysteriously with a startling tenderness. Then she immediately demanded to see what we had bought.

I handed her the paper bag Anne had laid on the table. She unwrapped the contents and evaluated, as an expert, the various advantages of the models we had chosen.

In doing this she used, as always, the most crude, humiliating terms, which never failed to bring a blush to the fresh face of her pupil. For my part, I was lost in admiration at the ingenuity at her command: only a woman would be able to hit upon the most vulnerable spots of her own sex with such knowing cruelty. The effect that her words had on me seemed to give me a glimpse of greater things to be expected from her in the future.

Then she asked me for an account of our shopping trip. I described briefly the high points of the scene in the fitting room and the deep impression made on our young salesgirl.

"And the little girl, did she behave herself?" Claire asked.

I made a face and shrugged as though I weren't quite sure, for suddenly I felt like exacting further tortures from our victim.

At this, Claire turned to her friend:

"You must have been happy, weren't you? To have everyone know what a little whore you are?" Then, more harshly, "Well, answer me!"

"Yes. . . I was happy. . . ."

"Happy about what?"

"I was happy . . . to show . . . how I had been whipped. . . ."

It was a barely audible murmur. Was she reciting something without understanding it, or was this what she really thought?

"You like being whipped?" her tormentor continued.

The obedient lips formed a silent "Yes."

"Stand up!" Claire ordered.

She was sitting opposite me. Anne, on my left between the two of us, stood up against the table. Her back was facing the rear wall. Claire went on:

"Put your hands on the table and lean forward. . . . Open your legs. . . . Bend your knees. . . ."

The girl carried out the orders.

Taking advantage of the fact that no one was

looking, Claire put her hand up under her dress, from behind. She announced the results to me at once:

"She's wet already, the little bitch! You only have to promise to whip her. . . . Would you like to see for yourself?"

I reached up, also, under the dress, and felt two agile fingers moving between the moist lips.

And again my eyes met Claire's, warm and conspiratorial, dreaming up the most terrible violences.

The waiter, a very young man, came to take our order. I was obliged to remove my hand.

Claire, on the contrary, had pushed her chair back against the wall to make her position seem more natural while continuing with her scandalous pursuit. Little Anne, panic-stricken, tried to straighten up. But she didn't have the courage to break away completely from her friend's attentions. So she stood there, desperately clinging to the table, staring in a daze at the dumfounded young man.

I took as long as possible giving all the details of our order. The waiter, I might add, didn't seem to hear me at all, for he couldn't take his eyes off the pretty girl with the distracted face, wide-eyed, lips parted, writhing in the grip of some invisible power across from him.

When I finally said:

"That will be all for the moment," he fled in terror. Claire, in a peaceful voice, asked:

"Well now, little one, does it feel nice?"

"Let me go, I beg of you," Anne implored all in one breath.

But Claire continued, saying:

"Which do you like better: when I embarrass you, or when I hurt you?" Then, turning to me, "Let's see, Jean, didn't you say that she wasn't good this afternoon?"

I affirmed that the girl indeed deserved a punishment. Claire didn't ask for an explanation. She probably knew only too well that it wasn't true.

"Good," she said, "then we're going to make her cry."

Anne's contortions became more and more painful. Her mistress was now torturing her under her dress.

After a few minutes, since a waiter was coming with our tray, she finally withdrew her hand.

"Don't think I'm letting you off so easily," she said. "When would you like to come over to my place, Jean?"

"Tomorrow evening," I said, "after dinner."

"Very well. It will be tomorrow, then. You may sit down."

The waiter, no longer the same young man as before, arranged the cups and plates and silverware on the table, paying no attention to us.

Claire sniffed her fingers, then put them under her friend's nose.

"Smell," she said, "see how good you smell."

The girl blushed again.

"Lick them!"

The girl opened her mouth and sweetly licked the finger tips impregnated with her own odor.

VIII

IN THE BATHROOM

The following evening, rue Jacob, I found Claire in her favorite indoor costume: tight pants and a narrow black sweater.

Her greeting struck me as being very impersonal, but no more so than usual, I suppose. At that time it was only when I was away from her that I could imagine her being more accessible. We sat down, each in one of the armchairs. I didn't ask where Anne was.

After exchanging a few remarks, of no real interest, I said:

"It's getting hotter and hotter outside. You might think it was the middle of August."

Claire looked at me with that somewhat distant, haughty expression that I had always known. Then, an idea apparently having crossed her mind, she gave me a friendlier, although ironical, smile, and answered:

"I regret, my dear, that we are obliged to keep

our clothes on. But in our role, you understand . . .
it's indispensable. . . ."

That word "our" sounded like a good omen.

"That's true," I said, "it's indispensable. . . . To
you especially, no doubt?"

She was willing to agree.

"Yes, perhaps, to me especially. . . ."

There was something like a hint of regret in her
words. At the same time her look grew vaguer, less
guarded. Once again I thought she might be stirred
by temptations of a different nature.

She was beautiful this way, much more beautiful.
. . . I hazarded an oblique approach:

"But all covered up like that, don't you ever get
too hot?"

Claire stared at me unflinchingly, and little by
little her features hardened. Then her eyes narrowed and the corners of her mouth turned down
in a parody of amused disdain:

"No, never," she said.

Then she got up from her chair:

"The little girl must be ready. Follow me!"

All her self-possession had returned.

The door that she opened, without knocking, led
into a room where I had never been before. It was
the bathroom.

Its vast dimensions, as well as its luxury, most unusual in these old apartment buildings, clearly indicated that it had been installed recently, probably by Claire herself. She must have sacrificed a whole room of the apartment to it.

In addition to the usual fixtures, in pale blue porcelain, I was struck at once by the presence of a couch, full-sized, in one of the corners. The bathtub was nearby, at right angles to the couch, against the far wall. It was an enormous bathtub, also pale blue, decorated like the walls with white ceramic tiles.

Anne was standing up in the bathtub facing the door, busy soaping her body with both hands.

Instinctively her hands, fingers spread, flew to her crotch and her breasts to cover them as much as possible. But a look from her mistress made her abandon this attempt at modesty. She took her little hands away, one after the other, with a frightened, constrained look, and finally stood with her arms at her sides, palms out, her head bent.

Her pink and blond flesh was glistening with soapsuds which had run together in places, forming trails of white bubbles. The delicate fullness of her body and her limbs cried out so to be touched that I could almost feel what that warm, wet, slippery embrace would be like, my hands sliding freely over the supple curves.

Claire gestured toward the couch where I stretched out, leaning on one elbow. Claire sat down across the opposite corner of the bathtub and said to her friend, who hadn't moved a muscle:

"Well, go ahead!"

The young girl began soaping herself again. But Claire, judging that she no longer had her heart in it, took charge of directing the action, indicating which areas should be scrubbed, which positions should be assumed (supposedly to make the job easier), and the whole scope and rhythm of the slightest movement.

The entire body was gone over, meticulously. From in front and behind, straight and bent over, one leg raised and the thighs opened wide, the hands at the back of the head caressing the neck, massaging the breasts, and lingering between the buttocks, all the motions of the bath had to be performed in front of us. Claire, of course, delighted in going back over the most intimate ones, the most indiscreet.

Two or three times, even, on the pretext of trying to make her directions clearer, Claire offered the assistance of her own expert fingers. She acquitted herself of this function with implacable gravity and preciseness which partly hid her mounting excitement. I had no trouble noticing, however, that she spoke and handled her pupil with more and more brutality.

As for the poor girl, she proved to be a model of docility even when forced to endure long, uncomfortable poses, excessive probings, or spectacular contortions.

When she was finally allowed to sink into the water for good, Claire, her sleeves rolled up, bent over the tub again to wash away, herself, the last traces of soap from the most secret recesses of the body. She took her time. Lying in the water, the body of her friend responded to her slightest touch, letting itself be rolled over and back, stretched out and bent up, opened and closed, with perfect flexibility and ease.

I edged up closer to the tub myself, without getting up from the couch. Anne's head happened to be at my end. Her mistress had ended up with both hands around her neck, squeezing it tighter and tighter, pretending to want to push her head under the water. . . .

Claire was smiling; but in the girl's green eyes a flicker of fear was growing which could only be real.

Nevertheless she obeyed the order to close her eyes, then to hide her hands behind her back in order to illustrate more clearly her role of the defenseless prey. . . . And Claire, very slowly, went on drowning her.

Anne gave herself up with complete abandon.

At that particular moment Claire's arms caught my attention. They were strong and well shaped, as I had imagined they would be. I wasn't prepared, however, to find them so graceful.

But Claire quickly realized that I was looking at her instead of at her victim. She stared back at me, pointedly, meaning to make me lower my eyes.

I smiled at her. . . . I told her that she had very attractive arms.

She let go her hold and stood up. As one might have guessed, her confusion only increased her violence toward little Anne.

"Get up!" she commanded.

As soon as the girl was on her feet she brutally made her open her legs and put her hands again behind her back.

"Don't move!"

Her lovely body was dripping, as well as her hair, which fell in sinuous strands over half her face and her neck.

Claire said, like a challenge:

"Would you like me to turn on the little fountain?"

"Why not?" I answered.

"All right, watch!"

She seized the dripping wet pubic hair in her hand and parted the lips to poke her fingers inside. In her haste she must have hurt the young woman, who winced. Claire ordered her to stand still, on pain of being further mistreated, then she said:

"Show the gentleman the pretty fountain."

However, her menacing tone did not suit the childish turn of the phrase at all.

The girl didn't have to be persuaded. She bent her knees slightly and threw out her chest. She closed her eyes. She steadied her arms in their position behind her back. The colorless liquid gushed out between Claire's fingers falling to the surface of the bath below with the sound of a rushing brook.

Claire played for an instant with the lips of the sex, and then with the stream itself, letting it land on her open hand which made it run down one of the thighs.

And I was, I admit, rather surprised at the charm of such a scene whose simple and wonderful sweetness filled me, even me, with pleasure.

IX

THE GOTHIC CHAMBER

Having washed the soiled body of her friend under a warm shower at great length, Claire, now full of little kindnesses and attentions, helped her get out of the bath. She dried her herself, rubbing, patting, polishing.

She brushed and combed the small triangle of pubic hair. Then she perfumed it with a vaporizer, also the breasts, the armpits, the neck, the underside of the buttocks and the groove between them.

While the girl's hair was drying, very quickly, thanks to a little electric dryer, she carefully applied a bright pink rouge to her mouth and the nipples of her breasts.

She seemed to be overflowing with tenderness, wondering what to think up next to further adorn the young woman, to set her off, pamper her. She didn't seem to mind kneeling in front of her, on the pale-blue, foam rubber rug, or kissing the favorite parts of her body whenever she wanted to.

As she accomplished these various jobs with the gestures of a mother, or a lady in waiting, or a child playing with a doll, she kept up a running commentary for my benefit, even asking my advice about which perfume to choose, or which shade of lipstick.

When all these things were finally finished she slipped on a pair of stockings with embroidered tops, and the white garter belt and bra that I had bought the day before. She made her masterpiece turn around for her, to give it one last final inspection, then she pushed it toward the couch:

"Go and kiss your master, who loves you."

The girl came and placed herself next to me, almost lying down, and kissed me for some time, with all the patience and gentleness I already knew were hers. I pressed my arm against her waist to hold her closer to me.

Then my hand crept up her back to her neck where it paused so that I could control the contact of our lips, their pressure, their timing, without having to move my own head. Unconsciously, the girl had begun to move her hips, a slow undulation that spread the length of her body, and of mine.

I suddenly wanted to look at Claire. I pushed away the blond head and laid the girl's face against my shoulder.

Claire's eyes went back and forth, from the pulsing hips to my hand, holding the neck in place, then to my eyes. Little Anne was now kissing me at the base of my neck.

I saw that her mistress was hurt by our embrace in which, suddenly, she had no part. I let her ordeal go on for a time. . . .

I let it go on, all the while looking at Claire, until she reached the end of her endurance. She was standing near the sofa, a few feet away, not knowing whether to separate us, or to join us.

When I finally freed myself, pushing the girl backward, Claire made her get up so that she could sit beside me herself:

"Come on, you little bitch, what do you think you're doing? Jean is here to watch you being tortured. You can kiss him later, if he feels like it, after we've made you suffer."

"Oh, that's right," I said calmly, "what are we waiting for, anyhow?"

As was customary, the victim had to kneel before her tormentors on the tiled floor to hear the particulars of the torture she would undergo.

She would be tied to one of the columns in the execution chamber. She would be whipped on the front of her thighs and on her lower belly. Then she would be burned with red-hot needles in the most sensitive parts of her body. And finally, her breasts would be whipped until they bled.

In a voice that was straining to sound natural, Claire asked me if I had ever used a certain kind of needle to torture a woman: "You'll see," she said, "it's most amusing. It hardly leaves a trace, and it's not at all dangerous since the point has been sterilized by the flame. But above all, it hurts terribly— isn't that right, little one?—and you can keep it up in the same place, without deadening the effect, indefinitely. . . ."

The Gothic chamber was exactly as it had been in the photographs: the iron bed, the paving stones in a black and white checkerboard pattern, the two stone pillars which supported a high vaulted ceiling above the narrow recessed window, covered now by red velvet curtains. The indirect lighting was diffused by brackets on the wall, and by three adjustable fixtures which threw their beams toward the ceiling. The whole thing, at once austere and intimate, reminded one vaguely of a chapel. This curious room certainly was not the most unexpected thing in the whole curious apartment.

There were also two leather armchairs in which we sat down, Claire and I.

Claire was thirsty. Obviously it was Anne who was sent to get the refreshments. She still wore the same things: the embroidered stockings (without shoes), the white nylon garter belt and bra whose styling obligingly left naked all that one would wish to see.

While we were drinking, the girl, who had had to serve us on her knees, was made to stay in that position until we had finished.

Her posture was the same one I had already had occasion to enjoy: thighs open, body very straight, arms raised, lips apart. Her large green eyes shone with a deep, almost supernatural brilliance that carried us back several centuries to the time of the ecstasies of the Christian martyrs.

We were aware, all three of us, that the tortures scheduled for the evening were by no means imaginary. The thought that they would, in a moment, wrench from this tender young girl the most voluptuous spasms of pain gave her flesh, which was desirable anyway, an incomparable allure. I made her come closer so that I could run my fingers over the curves and hollows which we were about to wound, with abandon, as long as it seemed entertaining.

Her sex was still moist, probably from our embrace in the bathroom; unless her humiliating posture, the immodesty that was required of her, or perhaps the anticipation of the torture, as Claire led one to believe, was enough to arouse her.

I felt like exciting her more by touching certain parts of her, but then I thought that it would be fun, in such a cruel situation, to make her do it herself.

"Supposing we made her play with herself first?" I said to Claire.

Claire, naturally, agreed. But she first wanted to put the black band over the girl's eyes. Anne, at the command, stood up to go and get the band, and also the whip, which were put away in a small chest in a corner of the room. After presenting them to her mistress, she resumed her former posture.

Claire showed the things to me. The whip was not the same one we had used the other day: instead of being braided it had a plain leather lash, more supple and cutting. Claire tried it out right away, on the girl's thighs. She winced, and turned her head to one side. A thin red line appeared on the smooth flesh.

"The little bitch chose a good one," Claire said. "She went and bought it herself, this morning."

With the help of a black velvet elastic ribbon Claire then masked her eyes, a charming finishing touch to her costume.

Still on her knees, one of the lights aimed at her, we made her caress herself: the upper parts of her breasts first, and their little rouged tips left exposed by her bra; then the interior of her sex under the arch of white nylon. She was made to use both hands, to open herself wide, at the same time hiding as little as possible from us with her fingers.

While this was going on we quietly finished our orangeade.

As though we had planned it, Claire and I turned to each other at the same moment. I was thinking of the last photograph, the one for which Anne had not been the model, which portrayed a similar scene.

I realized that Claire was thinking the same thing . . . and knew that I was thinking it. . . . Her face was in the shadows, but I could make out that same troubled expression, once again.

Anne couldn't see anything through her blindfold. I got up silently and leaned down over my neighbor's armchair. Her startled face was turned up to mine and I kissed it, scarcely brushing her lips, then covering her whole mouth, which began to soften. . . .

"Leave me alone," she suddenly cried out, standing up herself.

As an outlet for this emotion, which hadn't figured in her program, she turned on the kneeling girl. She seized the whip and began lashing her thighs, from in front, still not letting her interrupt her activities.

"Play with yourself, you whore!" Claire said, whipping her. Under the blows the girl instead stopped. Claire hit her again: "Go on, play with yourself!" The terrified girl began again at once. "Better than that!" Claire said, landing a sharp blow on her thighs.

Beyond endurance, Claire finally threw her to the floor and began furiously caressing her herself.

The girl was lying on her back, knees bent, arms flat on the floor on either side of her head. Claire was on one knee, leaning over her prey.

Almost immediately the girl began moaning. Soon she lost complete control, crying out continuously from deep inside her throat, her mouth wide open, her face thrown back.

"Look," Claire murmured, "how beautiful she is when she's coming, the little slut. . . ."

In effect, I saw the girl moving rhythmically, turning her head from one side to the other, clutching the floor with her fingers. Then, all in one motion, she stretched her legs out and rolled over on her side, bent double, motionless on the black and white floor.

Claire, standing over her, pushed her with the toe of her shoe, as though she were a corpse.

However, Claire still wasn't satisfied. She had to tear off the young woman's bra, her garter belt and her stockings, leaving only the black band across her eyes.

With strokes of the whip she made her get back on her knees in front of my chair. She gave the order to begin caressing herself again, adding one little refinement, humiliating, yet pleasurable:

"You're to play with your little asshole too, at the same time!"

Obediently, one of her hands went behind her back. This region must have been very sensitive, for she got excited at once.

But this time, instead of bringing her work to its

conclusion, Claire grabbed hold of the girl and dragged her over to one of the columns where she stood her, back against the stone. In a twinkling she had been tied up, arms and legs spread wide, hands and feet pulled backward.

I turned the lights in her direction and went closer. Her wrists and ankles were attached to two pairs of rings, diametrically opposed, by means of those flat leather bracelets that are sold in Parisian knickknack stores and affected by wives whose husbands love them. The upper rings were just at the right height (about six feet) to stretch the body as much as possible without hurting it.

Claire had begun her caresses again, savagely, penetrating her victim with such passion that one could no longer tell whether her cries were cries of pain or of pleasure.

There was no longer any doubt when Claire took up the flagellation again, striking the wide-opened thighs and the lower belly. The growing violence of her well-aimed blows, their accuracy and regularity, made the girl writhe in every direction in spite of the tightness of her bonds. Her body was so beautiful like this that my amazement grew as the sacrifice continued.

Exhausted, finally, Claire gave herself a rest and

took a moment to place a gag over her prisoner's mouth so that her screams wouldn't rouse the whole neighborhood.

Then she moved up within easy reach a little alcohol lamp which had been mounted on an iron stand so that it could be used conveniently. Once the flame was lit she propped her various instruments in it, which had special supports for this purpose.

I admired the long needles, sharpened to a fine point at one end and at the other fitted with wooden handles so that one could hold them without burning oneself. When the steel was red-hot, Claire undertook the skillful torture of first one breast, and then the other; then she operated on the inside of the thighs, at the very top where the whip hadn't reached.

She worked slowly, lovingly meting out the punishment: she began by a light touch on the surface of the skin, then, pressing harder and harder, ended up sinking the point about an eighth of an inch into the flesh.

The girl's desperate contortions interfered somewhat with her progress, but the groans of agony that could be heard even with the gag more than rewarded her efforts.

The victim's tears now flowed freely from under the blindfold down her cheeks. Her panting grew harsher. When Claire came back to the breasts, concentrating on the swelling near the armpit and the rouged area around the nipples, I thought the girl would break her arms and legs from pulling against the rings that held her spread-eagled on the column.

Then I took the whip and pushed Claire away so that I could administer myself the final punishment as promised, on the breasts. I contemplated the young woman, completely at my mercy, who had by now given up struggling or hoping for any reprieve.

And I whipped her with all my strength, reveling in it.

I only stopped when the delicate skin was broken and I could see a thin line of blood.

"Untie her," I told Claire. "Take off the bracelets . . . the gag . . . the blindfold . . . put her on the bed."

Little Anne lay still. She was on her right side facing the wall, her knees slightly bent. Her shoulders and buttocks had been bruised by the stone column during the course of the torture. I lay down beside her. I wrapped myself around her from behind, my body following the lines of her body. . . .

And I ravaged her, without any thought for her sufferings, penetrating the half-dead body through its smallest opening.

X

EVERYTHING RESOLVES ITSELF

That same night I had a dream. I was going into the Gothic chamber again, only it was larger and higher, like a church I remembered from my childhood.

A nude girl is tied to each of the two columns, one with her front toward me, the other her back. I come closer. I realize that they are both dead, but still warm. Their bodies have been pierced by many triangular stab wounds in the most propitious areas.

A little blood marks each wound. It is just starting to coagulate, I discover, touching it with my finger.

I lick my finger tip. The blood has a pleasant, sweetish taste: it might almost be a fruit syrup.

Then I notice another woman in front of a brilliant stained glass window in an archway at the back. She is dressed in voluminous, sumptuous materials, like the Madonnas of the Renaissance. She is seated on a throne, her arms held out in a queenly gesture of welcome. She has Claire's face. She is smiling gently at me but with a far-off, enigmatic smile.

As I walk toward her she seems to get farther and farther away.

I woke up, smiling to myself at this dream with its allegorical aspects but with no real meaning. I nevertheless had the feeling that I was expecting a visit from Claire, even though she hadn't breathed a word about it the night before.

When I heard the doorbell ring, a little later, I knew at once that it was she. I threw a bathrobe over my pajamas, which I'd put on again after washing, and went to the door.

Claire was pale, a little tired looking. She had the beauty of a trapped wild animal.

"Good morning," I said to her. "How is your friend feeling?"

She didn't ask me, this time, which friend I was referring to.

Anne was feeling fine. She was still sleeping, worn out from the evening before. Claire had cared for her like a mother and in a few days nothing would show at all. Except, perhaps, a little red line on her breast where the skin had been broken.

"That would be a shame. . . ."

"Oh no," she said, "it will be very pretty."

She spoke softly, a little anxiously, not daring to look me in the face. We were still standing in the entrance, and I wasn't at all sure yet why she had come.

"And you," I asked, "how are you feeling?"

She stared at me wide-eyed, with a look of abandon; then lowered her eyelids before answering me.

"I have come," she said quietly.

"Good," I said. "Follow me."

Once in the bedroom I sat down in a chair and looked at her. She was standing near the bed, wearing a pleated skirt and a white blouse.

Then, I gave the order:

"Get undressed!"

She only hesitated for a second. She knelt in front of me on the sheepskin rug and began to take her clothes off, one by one, according to the ritual. Her underclothes were exactly like her protégée's. She, too, wore no panties.

When she was completely naked she spread her knees apart and raised her arms above her head.

I let her stay in this position for several minutes.

"Look at me!"

She lifted her eyes to me again.

"You like being on your knees?"

She said "Yes" by a nod of her head, and then murmured: "I am yours. . . . You can do whatever you want with me. . . ."

"That's good," I said. "Go and lie down on the bed."

She lay down on her back across the rumpled sheets.

"Open your legs! . . . Hands behind your back! . . . Mouth open! . . ."

Without a word, she obeyed.

I got up, took off my clothes, and half lay on top of her body. I put a hand under the back of her neck to hold her.

"You've never been beaten?"

She shook her head, her eyes melting in anguish.

"Well then, that makes me the first one."

I slapped her, to the right, to the left, once, twice. I looked at her for a long time and then told her she was beautiful.

My hand traveled down her belly and I thrust my thumb directly into her sex. It was as wet as possible. . . .

I kissed her, caressing her all the while.

Then I raised myself on one elbow and slapped her again, much harder, five or six times.

"Say 'I love you,' " I commanded.

She repeated: "I love you," adding that she was my slave and I could beat her to death if it would amuse me.

I caressed her breasts, then her sex, at greater length and with more precision. Afterward I made her lick my fingers.

When I penetrated her for good she began to cry out, calling me by my first name and repeating over and over that she loved me. . . .